A Tree for Peter

A TREE FOR PETER

WRITTEN AND ILLUSTRATED BY

Kate Seredy

New York

THE VIKING PRESS

PRINTED IN THE UNITED STATES OF AMERICA

SECOND PRINTING NOVEMBER 1941
THIRD PRINTING MARCH 1946
FOURTH PRINTING AUGUST 1950
FIFTH PRINTING MARCH 1954
SIXTH PRINTING OCTOBER 1959

J

Published on the same day in the Dominion of Canada by
The Macmillan Company of Canada Limited
First published in October 1941

To Nicholas;
to the magic light of
the tiny Christmas candle
in his hands
and the one who keeps it burning:
Anne Carroll Moore

The Boy in Shantytown

Tommy was six years old when he first saw Shantytown. He had never before seen anything so sad and ugly. He saw it through a train window on a rainy afternoon. The rain ran like rivulets of tears off the half-blind old windows of the crooked old houses and off their crooked old roofs that looked like shapeless hats. The houses in Shantytown were sort of huddled together around a taller one that looked like a church. It had a small steeple and a tall, broad doorway that gaped wide open. But it had no glass in its windows and there were no lights inside. There were no lights in any of the houses. The train was going very slowly and Tommy could have seen right through the windows, had there been lights inside. But all the windows were dull with dirt and dark. Many of them were stuffed with rags and papers where the glass had broken.

Beyond the crooked old houses Tommy could see a rust-eaten iron fence and below that, deep down below, ran the river the train had followed all afternoon. There was another fence, a tall, new, black-painted iron fence close to the railroad tracks. The train had stopped and then Tommy saw the boy. He stood by the new fence, looking at the train. He was very thin and pale. His clothes were barely more than rags, and they too were dripping with rain. His blond hair was streaming and big drops were running down his face as if he were crying. But he wasn't. Tommy pressed closer to the window and saw that the boy was looking right at him and smiling just a little. He smiled back and waved. Then he said: "Go home, boy. You will catch cold without your rubbers on."

Tommy's father looked up from the newspaper he was reading. "Whom are you talking to, Tommy?"

"The nice boy," said Tommy. "He is very wet."

Tommy's mother came across the aisle. "What a dreadful place!" she exclaimed. "Do people live here?"

"Tramps, bums, and derelicts," said Tommy's father, with a shrug. "Every big city has a dump like this, a Shantytown."

The train began to move again and the boy took a few steps along the fence, still looking at Tommy. Tommy saw that he was limping. "He is lame!" he exclaimed.

"Who is lame, Tommy?" asked his father.

"The nice boy. He is all alone and he is wet and lame. But he is not a bum," he added defensively.

[2]

His father glanced out, but by that time the train had moved away. "I didn't see anyone. Come, Tommy, look out on the other side. You can see the skyscrapers and the bay with the lighted ships."

Tommy turned and looked out of the window on the other side of the train. There was the big city, spread out before him, rows upon rows upon rows of lighted windows shining in the dark gray afternoon. Lights danced on the wet pavements below and lights shone from thousands of windows high above. Skyscrapers outlined in lights like diamonds against the dark gray sky and great ships outlined in many-colored lights against the stormy gray water in the bay. Here was the magic city, the city of lights, just as his father said it would be. It was so beautiful that in a little while Tommy forgot the lame boy who was alone in dark, sad Shantytown. He didn't remember him again for a long, long time, because the big city was so full of fun and excitement. When the time came to go home to the small town where they lived, they went a different way. So Tommy didn't see Shantytown again.

But he didn't really forget the boy in Shantytown. The boy was always there, deep inside Tommy's heart, standing alone in the rain, smiling a little smile. For years and years the boy and the dark, ugly houses behind him were merely silent pictures in Tommy's heart. Then one day he knew that all the time they were trying to say something to him. It was the day when Tommy was graduated from high school. His friends were discussing what they were going to do, now that school was over. Some were going to college, others wanted to learn a trade; there were some who were to be farmers and some who couldn't decide.

"And you, Tommy?" They asked him about his plans. Tommy was silent for a little while because he was listening to voices inside him. The lonely boy was there and he seemed to say: "I am cold and alone. I want a home . . . a house, a friendly house. But I am poor and there is no room for me in a friendly house. . . ." And the dark old houses seemed to say: "We are sad and lonely. We want happy children to live in our rooms, children who laugh and play, and then run home to us when they are tired. But we are ugly and old and only those who have no place to go come to live where we are. . . ."

Tommy was silent for so long that one of his friends shook him, laughing. "Tommy! Have you gone to sleep? We asked you what you were going to do?" And Tommy said: "I was . . . I was just remembering that . . . that I want to be a builder."

More years went by while Tommy grew to be a man, while he worked and learned to be a builder. He was so busy, he all but forgot about the lonely boy in Shantytown.

Then one day he was on the train again, going, for the second time in his life, to the big city. He was a grown man now and his name had grown up too. In his home town people knew him as Mr. Thomas Crandon, the builder. He was on his way to meet another builder, whose name was Peter Marsh. Peter Marsh was

[4]

famous. He had done what Thomas Crandon wanted to do: he had built hundreds of houses, whole big blocks full of honest, tight, good little houses. They were all built for poor people. Thomas Crandon wanted to talk to him; to find out how to build good, friendly houses for little money. He wanted poor people in his own home town to have the best houses he could build for them.

Some time in the afternoon the train found the river again and from then on they ran a race toward the big city. Thomas Crandon folded his newspaper and sat close to the window. He watched the race between the river and the train, just as he had done when he was six-year-old Tommy. He remembered every bend and curve; the place where the river widened and put two arms around a small green island and the tiny stations the train whistled at and left behind without stopping. Then the train slowed down and there was the tall, new, black-painted iron fence close to the tracks. Thomas Crandon pressed his face to the windowpane because he suddenly remembered again, for the first time in many years, the little lame boy who stood alone in sad, old Shantytown.

But where was Shantytown? Here was the strip of land between the tracks and the steep riverbank; here was the cluster of houses around the tiny church. But they were brave and gay with fresh white paint. Their windows, clean and whole, were like shining eyes through which he could see friendly rooms. Each house stood on a gay carpet of garden and beyond, the rusty fence was gone. Broad white steps wound down along the bank to a boat-landing, where rowboats and canoes tugged at their ropes. And everywhere were children, shouting, laughing, racing across the lawns, and none of them was lame.

There was a new round clock in the steeple of the church, its hands straight up and down, saying just six o'clock. Above the clock a golden bell began to ring, twinkling in and out of its own little house. A straight, tall pine stood guard on the lawn in front of the church door, its slim top reaching almost as high as the steeple.

"But where is Shantytown?" asked Thomas Crandon, speaking aloud in surprise.

"You are looking at it, Mister—or what *was* Shantytown," said the porter behind him. "Now it's called Peter's Landing, for Mr. Peter Marsh."

"Peter Marsh!" exclaimed Thomas Crandon, turning around quickly. But there was no time for all the questions he wanted to ask because the conductor called: "Last stop. Central Terminal." The train slid into a tunnel and in a few minutes Thomas Crandon was walking toward his hotel in the big city.

"Tomorrow," he said to himself, "tomorrow I am going to ask Peter Marsh just what magic he used to change sad, ugly Shantytown into beautiful Peter's Landing."

Next day he went to see Peter Marsh. From the moment the two men shook hands, they talked and felt as if they had been friends for a long, long time. By late afternoon the large desk between them and the floor around were littered with plans, blueprints, and pictures of small, good little houses. They had finished with business and now they were just talking like the old friends both felt they were. Thomas Crandon was telling about his first trip to the city, when he was six-year-old Tommy; about the rainy afternoon when he saw the lame boy who stood in the rain and smiled.

"And you know," he said, "I didn't know then, but I do know now that I have become a builder because"—he hesitated—"well, because I felt so sorry for those old crooked houses and the lonely boy. And today," he said, smiling, "I want to know just what magic you have used to change that dreary place into the smiling spot now called Peter's Landing . . . for you, as I heard on the train."

Peter Marsh looked at him intently and for a moment he didn't answer. Then he said slowly: "Magic. Yes, it was magic that made Peter's Landing. But the magic was not of my making and it is not called Peter's Landing for me. I named it for a friend, whose name was also Peter. King Peter. He held the magic wand. It was . . . it was a spade," he added with a chuckle.

"A . . . a . . . spade?" asked Thomas Crandon in wonder. "And King Peter . . . ! It sounds like a story."

"A spade. A little toy spade with a red handle from the five-and-ten-cent store," said Peter Marsh quietly. "It is a story. A long one. About a lame boy, a little red spade, a tiny Christmas tree, and a . . . a man nobody knew. Want to hear it?"

"Please."

Peter Marsh leaned back in his chair. The desk was a pool of

[7]

light under the green-shaded lamp but beyond it the room was growing dark. The voice of Peter Marsh came from the shadows of the darkening room and as he began his story, Thomas Crandon felt that he was six-year-old Tommy again, seeing for the first time sad old Shantytown.

A Friend for Peter

On a narrow strip of land between the river and the railroad tracks stood the old house where small Peter lived. It did not stand alone, for, if it had, the winds would have blown it down long ago. It was one of a cluster of forlorn houses huddled together around a taller one that once had been a church. Between them was a yard so full of rubbish that not even a blade of grass could grow among the junk. The houses were nobody's houses. No one remembered the people who had built them and no one cared. No one ever claimed rent from those who came to take shelter under their leaking roofs.

Along the riverbank ran a rust-eaten fence. It may have been a garden fence, but now there was no garden left to guard; only a dump where people threw the things they could no longer use. It was a silent place, that poor, dreadful yard. People who lived around it lived behind closed shutters and shades tightly drawn. They were trying to hide, even from one another, how very poor they were. Close neighbors though they were, not one of them knew or cared what ill luck had forced the rest to live around a dump. They were too poor to care for anything but daily bread. They had nothing to share, not even hope for better days to come.

Each dawn they left for the city, in search of work. They always went alone, one by one, silent, lone shadows drifting across the tracks. At night they drifted back, one by one, clutching small parcels of food or cast-off clothing, but often they came with empty hands.

Small Peter's mother was one of them. She was a sad, tired woman who seldom smiled. Small Peter knew she worked in a laundry. Her hands were dry and wrinkled and she always smelled of soap. On weekdays he hardly saw her; she left at daybreak while he was still asleep. At night she was so tired she often fell asleep over their meager meal. Sundays were different. On warm Sunday afternoons they walked away from Shantytown, along the rusty fence, hand in hand. They sat on the high riverbank in the sun. Then she would hold him close and tell him stories. She talked of many things.

She told him of the house where they used to live before his father died. A white house surrounded by a garden all fresh and green under the friendly trees. Of kittens romping on the lawn and a brown, silky dog who wagged his tail. But mostly she talked of the strong, kindly man she called Daddy and whom Peter remembered as someone in a dream. Her stories were all like dreams to Peter. He always sat very still to make them last. He didn't want Sunday to end, because then Monday would come and he would be alone again and afraid.

He was afraid of many things.

There were other boys who lived in Shantytown; loud, rough boys who could jump and run and who laughed at him because he was slow and lame. He was glad when they clambered down the rocks to the river or ran across the tracks to play wild games in the field beyond. He knew they didn't want him and he didn't like their games or the ugly things they said. So most of the time he kept hidden in the house, until they went away.

He was afraid of the lean, hungry cats that came to prowl among the junk. Afraid of the rats they sometimes chased. Afraid of the dogs with yellow eyes and tails that never wagged. They, poor, homeless beasts, were more afraid of him than he was of them, but he didn't know that. He kept very still when one of them came to the yard, until it went away.

He was afraid of summer's thunderstorms and the icy winds of winter, angry winds that tore shingles from the rooftops and howled down the chimney.

Small Peter, lame and lonely, was afraid of many things that came to Shantytown, but mostly of Him, the big policeman.

There was too much of Him. He was too tall, too wide across the middle, He was too new, too freshly scrubbed. His voice was too loud. It rolled like thunder and made small Peter shrink, although His words were kind:

"Hi, Peanut. What is the news today?"

It was an idle question. Peter shook his head and whispered: "Nothing." What could he say? There were no news in Shantytown. None that a small boy could tell a big policeman, a COP. Even the rough boys who could jump and run were afraid of Him. Small Peter heard them yell: "Beat it! Here comes the cop."

He couldn't run away, so he merely stood and waited until at last He turned and went away. He always frowned and grumbled while He walked around the old houses. He called them dirty shacks. He grumbled to Himself, but Peter heard Him. His words were like cruel flashes of lightning. They made small Peter see the hopeless ugliness of Shantytown.

Day after day they met, and parted. It was always the same. "Hi, Peanut. What is the news today?" "Nothing."

There was nothing new in Shantytown.

Then, one day when Peter was almost six years old, something did happen in Shantytown that was new to Peter.

He found a friend.

It happened on a chilly afternoon in early spring. The house was cold with all the winter frost still in its rattling bones. Peter wandered out into the sunshine, seeking a sheltered spot where the wind would not find him. He wandered from place to place, but the wind was everywhere. It howled at him from around corners, it laughed when it poked cold fingers through his threadbare coat.

And then, above the shrill voice of the wind he heard another sound. Someone was whistling a merry tune. It came from the yard, from among tin cans, broken bottles, rusty, twisted shapes which once were beds and springs. Peter had never before ventured into the heart of this dreadful yard; he was afraid of the queer, tortured shapes of once-useful things. Now it seemed like an adventure to follow the call of that merry tune.

Rounding the bulky shape of an old rusty stove he stumbled on a wire and fell almost into the lap of a strange man, a man who was to be his friend.

"Huh!" The man jumped to his feet with a startled grunt. Sharp words were ready on his tongue but the sharp words were never spoken. He looked at Peter's thin face and startled eyes and his own eyes crinkled into a smile. "You frightened me, boy. I thought nobody lived here."

"I do," said Peter. "In there," he added, pointing behind him to the house. The man sat down again, crosslegged on the ground. He had made a small heap of twigs, rags, and papers and now he held a match to it. The fire flared up.

"I am cold," he said, rubbing his hands together.

"So am I," said Peter. The man untied the string that held his coat together where buttons should have been and spread it out like a tent. "Sit down."

Peter crawled under the coat. It closed around him, shutting out the wind. He was not afraid. He felt safe in the shelter of this strange man's coat. He could not see the dreadful yard, only the friendly fire. He could not hear the wind, only a quiet voice asking:

"You . . . live here alone?"

"With my mother on Sundays. Weekdays I live alone."

"No father?"

"No. He died."

There was a short silence. Then the man said: "That's tough. A fellow wants a man to talk to."

Peter thought this over and found it was true. He looked at the man and smiled. "You are a man. I like to talk to you."

"Thank you. So do I," said the man.

Peter sighed and snuggled deeper into the shelter of the coat. It was ragged and gray with age, just like his own. This man was not new and loud like the big policeman; everything about him was worn. His eyes were wrinkled and his cheeks deeply seamed. His hair was gray and limp under a sagging hat. His voice was as faded as his coat, but it was as comforting and warm too.

"What is your name?" Peter wanted to know.

"It used to be King, Mr. Peter King, when I still had a name. I lost it somewhere along the road. Now people call me Tramp."

"I like your lost name better," said small Peter thoughtfully. "That is my name too but I am not a Mr. King. I . . . I am . . . lame," he added, looking fearfully into the face above him to see if it made a difference. But the tired eyes only smiled more tenderly and the man said:

"You are a prince, Peter. There is a story about a little prince, you know, whose foot was lame. He could not run away when he was in danger or afraid. He learned never to be afraid of anything and grew into the bravest man . . . just because he was lame and could not run. Are you afraid of things, Peter?"

Peter felt very brave in the shelter of the coat. He was ready to say: "No, I am not afraid," but the words caught in his throat. Behind the rusty stove a shadow moved and two yellow eyes stared into his own.

"The dog, Mr. Peter . . ." he whispered, pointing with a shaking finger. The man turned his head.

"Poor thing," he said, "look how it trembles. Be kind to it, Peter; it's only a homeless dog." He lowered his voice to a soothing murmur as he spoke to the dog:

"Come here, pal; come. We will not hurt you. Come like a good dog. Come. . . ."

It came. A timid wag began at the tip of its tail, then slowly it crept out of the shadow of the stove, toward the fire and the voice that was so kind. Inch by inch it edged closer, half eager, half afraid. It began to whine in thin, broken little sobs and now its tail wagged much faster, thumping the ground.

"That's the good dog. . . . Come closer. Come . . ." the tramp said, and small Peter chimed in: "Good dog, come closer . . . don't be afraid."

With an effort that made its whole thin body tremble, the dog overcame whatever terror human nearness held for it. It whined again as if asking for mercy, then thrust its head under Peter's out-stretched hand. Peter, holding his breath, moved shy fingers down its scrawny neck. It looked up and whined.

"Good dog," said the tramp very softly. The dog sighed a deep sigh and lay down, in utter confidence, on the torn edge of the coat.

"You see, Prince Peter," said Peter the tramp, with a smile, "we didn't run from this shadow and we found that it was nothing but a homeless dog wanting a little kindness."

Peter thought this over and found it was true. The discovery gave him a light, bubbly feeling inside. It was his Sunday feeling: a funny little tickle that made him want to sing and laugh.

The Sunday feeling did not leave. Not even when, at sundown, his friend went away. The Sunday feeling stayed because Mr. Peter had promised to come again.

The dog, whom they named Pal, stayed too. Not openly, like a house dog; he did not sleep on the doorstep, nor did he ask Peter for food. But every time Peter was all alone, he appeared from somewhere. Together they waited for Mr. Peter to call them with his merry tune, as he promised he would. They waited day after day and each day was a little longer, for spring had come, then turned into summer.

And then, on a morning in early June, Pal lifted both his ears, barked a short "Come on" to Peter, and bounded away. He raced back and forth along the rusty fence, found the hole where most of the fence's teeth were gone, crawled out and down the ledge. From deep down below came the merry tune.

Peter had never before ventured down this rocky bank where only fearless boys who were not lame played. But now there was the tune to follow and Pal, his dog, leading him on to meet their friend.

Small Peter started down the ledge. And as he went, he saw that there was a path between the rocks; a steep path, to be sure, but once he found it, he had nothing to fear.

The path wound steeply down between the rocks and boulders. The rocks had looked dangerous from above, but now that Peter was among them they turned out to be friends. They supported him from left and right, so he could not slip and fall; they kept him from seeing too far ahead, so he would not get dizzy.

They kept the secret of a surprise waiting for Peter until he reached the end of the path. There, on the tiny, pebbly beach Peter did not need them, for Mr. Peter was on the beach and beside him was a boat. A small boat, painted white and green.

"Oh!" was all Peter could say. Mr. Peter held out his hands and swung Peter onto his shoulder. "We are going fishing today," he said, so simply that all the endless yesterdays while Peter waited for him to come seemed like no time at all.

Then they were floating on the shining little waves, small Peter and his friend, with Pal between them. Peter's heart was bursting with the Sunday feeling. He had no words to go with the way he felt; all the words he knew seemed dull and gray. The Sunday feeling was bright as the sunshine and sharp as the little waves around the boat. It would not stay down but spread into Peter's cheeks, making them pink and hot; it crept into his eyes, making them shine like stars, and finally it burst out into a laughing sentence:

"The sun is dancing inside me, Mr. Peter!"

Mr. Peter knew the word to go with the Sunday feeling. He said, smiling at Peter:

"I am happy too."

Forever after, the memory of that happy day remained in Peter's heart. It was a secret treasure he could not talk about even to his mother. Each hour of that day was like a precious jewel he could

pick up and gaze at when he was alone. Each hour was a different color but all were bright.

There was the quiet green hour in the shady cove across the river.

Soft green grass underfoot, moist and cool to roll on.

Whispering green trees above, their leaves cutting the glaring sun into cool shafts of light.

Cool water lapping the shore, a deep, dark green mirror of water to gaze into and see a laughing boy, or to wade into and see the shining minnows dart between his feet.

There was the hour that was all silver sparkle, when the big fish he caught slashed through the water swiftly like a knife and when it plunged again and again and showered a fountain of sparkling spray on Peter, when Pal, yelping with joy, plunged in too to catch the leaping fish, but couldn't, and when Mr. Peter scraped the fish, hard, silver scales jumping around his knife. . . .

There was the magic red hour around the fire in the cove. First, there was fish to eat, roasted in the embers; there were juicy red tomatoes and firm apples and, later, a good, full feeling around his middle that made Peter drowsy.

Soft red lights danced up and down the tree-trunks, touched Pal's silky ears and threw a scarlet cloak around Mr. Peter. Above his head a shaft of sun had found an opening and changed his gray, windblown hair into a crown of gold. Peter gazed at him sleepily.

"Now you look like a king."

Mr. Peter smiled. "Have you ever seen a king, small Peter?"

"I have, on the picture my mother keeps in a book. There is a man on the picture. He is standing alone, under a tree. He has a light around his head, like you, and his face is . . . good. My mother said he was a king. . . . You are a king too. King Peter."

The voice of his friend was very soft when he said: "Maybe I am. A mighty king in disguise whom no one may see, only Prince Peter, his friend."

"And Pal," whispered Peter, closing his eyes. "Pal knew you had come even before I heard you. King Peter . . . he . . . loves you . . . too. . . ."

A gentle hand on his hair was the last thing Peter remembered of the magic red hour. He slept.

There was the hour, later, that was not a color but a sharp, clean smell. It was the smell of fallen leaves and the smell of freshly turned earth, where Peter's friend had been digging for worms; where Peter burrowed among the leaves to search for funny bugs he had never seen before. The flat, gray ones that crawled from under stones he didn't care for and the black ones that looked like roaches in Shantytown he hated. But there were round red ones dotted with black, there were squarish ones striped yellow and green, long, narrow bugs with shiny coats, stiff and hard to the touch.

Peter lay on his stomach, his face close to the ground. He saw a green beetle emerge from under a leaf. It had brilliant black eyes and a brown head with quivering feelers stuck in it like jaunty feathers. It climbed onto a yellow leaf and began to wash its face. It sat so close to Peter's eyes that suddenly it didn't look like a bug at all, but a little man wearing a crown of brown velvet and a stiff coat of green silk.

"Here is the King Bug!" yelled Peter. But when his friend came to look, there was nothing to see but a yellow leaf.

"I did see the King Bug!" insisted Peter, then smiled gaily at his friend. "But I guess he was in disguise too, and no one can see a king in disguise but me, Prince Peter."

There were the birds to remember, all colors of the rainbow, and the sweet music they made.

[34]

There was the fresh little rabbit that peeked from behind a tree-trunk, all fuzzy ears and shining eyes. Pal chased it back into the woods and the rabbit's bobbing little white tail looked so funny that Peter had to laugh until he ached all over.

Then, going homeward in the boat, there was the blue hour, when all around was water, blue as the sky above and just as deep, when long, plum-colored shadows crept softly across the water from the shore the boat was leaving.

And then, almost at sunset, King Peter began to speak and what he said changed sad, ugly Shantytown into a castle and the big policeman into a friend.

In the middle of the river King Peter held his oars and said:

"Do you know that you live in a golden castle, Prince Peter?"

Peter shook his head sadly. "Oh, no. Where I live is a dirty shack. He said so."

King Peter frowned. "And who may He be?"

"The big policeman with the buttons and the stick." Peter shuddered and added resentfully: "He calls me Peanut."

"Hmmm," said King Peter. "Is he tall and broad, with a red face and stiff brushes for eyebrows?"

Peter nodded. "And he uses angry words like 'dirty shacks' and 'dump' and 'dele . . . de . . . derelicts.' "

"Did he call you that?" asked King Peter quickly.

"No. He just says: 'Hello, Peanut. What is the news today?' Then after a while he goes away to scold all by himself."

"And what do you say to him?"

"Nothing. I just wait until he goes away."

"I see," said King Peter quietly. "I didn't think you could frighten a big policeman like Patrolman John Patrick O'Flanahan of Precinct Fifty-Two."

Peter giggled. "Patrolman . . . Pat . . . what?"

"His friends call him Pat. He is the best man on the force, but you scared him."

"How?" Peter wanted to know.

"Well, he comes to you all the way from the city, just to pay you a visit, to see that you are well and safe. He comes and says hello, nice and polite, he asks for the news of the day. He is tired from the long walk, he would like to sit down and talk to you—but he can't."

"Why can't he?" asked Peter, beginning to feel sorry for Pat.

"Suppose you went to his house and said: 'Hello, Pat,' friendly and polite, and he would not answer at all, would *you* stay?"

"N - no."

King Peter went on: "Now, if I were you, I would sort of wait for him and when he comes I would call: 'Hello there, Pat!' and I would ask him to sit down and rest his feet. . . ."

"Would you, King Peter?"

"Indeed I would."

"Well, then . . . I guess I will too. 'Hello there, Patrolman . . . Say it again, please."

[38]

"Patrolman John Patrick O'Flanahan of Precinct Fifty-Two, the best man on the force."

Peter laughed. "His name is long enough to go around him where he is widest. I will just call him Pat."

King Peter nodded. "That's right. And now look at your castle, my Prince." He pointed across the river, to the rocks on which stood Shantytown. What Peter saw there made him gasp with wonder and surprise. From the shadowy riverbed rose the dark, steep wall of rocks and on the rocks stood a golden castle against the pale blue sky. A castle of many roofs and many windows gleaming in the last rays of the setting sun.

It was the golden hour.

After that, there was only the end of day to remember.

Peter and his friend stood on the tiny, pebbly beach, now purplish gray in the shadow of the rocks. High overhead a golden streak of sunlight was waiting for Peter.

"It will be much easier to go up, now that you know the path," said King Peter quietly.

"I know. I am not afraid," said Peter, then touched King Peter's hand. "King Peter . . ."

"Yes, my Prince?"

"I would like to . . . dig in the yard, like you did for worms. I don't want worms"—he shuddered a little—"I just want to . . . to dig up that good smell . . . the earth. It smelled so good . . . not like the . . . stuff in the yard."

"I know," King Peter said. "I will bring you a spade. A shiny, new spade with a red handle."

"When?" asked Peter eagerly.

"You will find it in the yard tomorrow. Good night now, Prince Peter. Wave to me when you get up to the castle."

The friendly rocks were there to help Peter along the path, then there was the rust-eaten fence at the end. Before he crawled after Pal into the yard, he turned and waved. Below him all was purple darkness; the happy day and King Peter were gone, but the golden sun was around him and on the houses, and soon, very soon, tomorrow would come.

It was Pal who found the spade next morning. When everyone was gone and Peter was alone in Shantytown, Pal came bounding from the yard. He called Peter. He called him with his ears and eyes and his wagging tail. He barked his sharp "Come on," and trotted ahead of Peter, back to the yard. By the rusty stove he stopped and looked at Peter wisely, as if to say: "Here it is."

There, leaning against the stove, was the spade. It was shiny new, with a red handle: Peter's hands closed around it. It felt good, all clean and new; it had a good smell of wood and paint and it was beautiful. It was the first new thing Peter had ever had. He hugged it. Something very good was happening to him again, way inside; and again he had no words for it. Years later he knew that the little red spade had been a tool to the boy Peter, a toy to the

child he was; it was a sword to fight ugliness with . . . but at the moment it was only a shiny spade, clean, unused, all his own.

He began to dig, shoving aside the rubbish that was between him and the dark, moist earth. Pal cocked his head aside and sniffed. He could not smell anything worth digging for like a rabbit or even a rat, but his small friend was laughing and that meant that something good was going on. So he began to dig too, dog-fashion, with his paws.

And right there the magic began.

They were simply playing, little lame Peter and Pal, a stray; they had no way of knowing that each fresh clump of earth they turned up was far more than earth. They had begun to bury sad Shantytown and to build Peter's Landing.

A Spade for Peter

Peter was singing. It was not just a song; it was the Sunday feeling called happiness coming out loud, as loud as he could shout. Pal was singing too, dog-fashion, in sharp yipping barks. Between them, they made so much noise that they didn't hear any-one coming until He, the big policeman, was standing right next to them. He looked funny. His eyebrows were way up on his forehead and his mouth was a round O of surprise. It grew still rounder when Peter shouted:

"Hello there, Patrolman John Patrick O'Flani . . . Flana . . . Anyway, look at my spade!"

In a moment Pat's kindly Irish face was beaming. "Bless my soul, the laddie has come alive!" he exclaimed. "Peanut, me lad, and what is it you are doing?"

"Digging with my spade," said Peter, then touched Pat's hand with a tentative finger. "You say the rest, O'Flani . . . what?"

"Just call me Pat, laddie," replied Pat, beaming.

"Sit down, Pat, and rest your feet," said Peter, remembering what his friend would have said.

"They sure are tired, laddie," sighed Pat, lowering his bulk, spotless blue coat and all, onto the rusty stove. "Beautiful dirt that is," he said, looking at the glistening clumps. "I recall when I was a wee lad in Ireland . . . I used to grub in the good, clean dirt and love the good, clean smell of it. Ah . . . a happy lad I was in Ireland. . . ."

[46]

"You can have my spade to dig now," said Peter, offering his treasure and with it his heart.

Pat hugged Peter to him. "Bless your heart, laddie . . ." he began, but got no farther. Pal, who had been sniffing at him from a comfortable distance, now rose to protect his small friend from this big stranger. He growled a warning growl. Pat held Peter a little closer and lifted his stick to chase the dog away. But his hand came down again slowly and gently because Peter repeated words that had brought him comfort:

"Don't be afraid, Pat; be kind to him and he will be your friend."

Pat looked from one to the other in silence. He must have wanted to laugh at the thought that he, a big Irish policeman, would be afraid of anything. But he didn't laugh. Instead he said to Peter: "Forgive me, laddie. I have a lot to learn from the likes of you." To Pal he held out a hand and said: "Come here, old boy; you won't find an Irishman lacking in kindness." Pal believed him. He came and allowed Pat to scratch him behind his ears.

"You see, Pat," said Peter seriously, "there was nothing to be afraid of. You scare too easy. You were afraid of me too. I know!"

Pat could hold his laughter no longer. It popped out and shook him like a storm. It was a big, hearty laugh, the kind Peter had never heard before. His own laughter rang out in answer and Pal laughed too, dog-fashion. Shantytown's old houses echoed the sound of friends laughing together.

[48]

After that, the big policeman came every day, as before. Only now he was not He, the big policeman, just Pat, a friend. He was full of good, rumbling laughter and of stories. He told Peter of Ireland, where the hills were a checkerboard of green grass and sky-blue flax, where white cottages peeked from under their thatched roofs like small boys in need of a haircut, where wee folk lived in the hollows of trees and under the hedgerows.

He told Peter of the wide ocean he had crossed on a ship bigger than all of Shantytown; of the great harbor in New York, where countless ships, big and small, rushed back and forth like water-bugs in a pond. He spoke of the city where everything was made of stone, concrete, and steel; where lights were too bright and shadows far too black, where motors and machines roared day and night on the streets and underground and even winged ones, called airplanes, in the sky. Where a policeman had friends in every house on every street he walked and yet had no one to love. Where an Irish policeman could walk the hard, icy streets in winter and the hard, burning streets in summer and never see a hollow tree that wee folk could hide in. Where a policeman could only dream of owning a spot of land big enough to turn a spade in, to drop a seed in and watch it grow into something green and alive.

Peter loved to listen. Each day Pat's stories brought something new to Shantytown. No longer were the railroad tracks the end of the world for Peter. Pat's stories were like paths on which Peter's dreams could travel into the world beyond the tracks.

[50]

Sometimes Pat took the little spade into his big mitts of hands and, carefully so as not to break the tiny tool, dug up a little spot. Then one day he just stood gazing at the freshly turned ground. His eyes lighted up with a sudden thought and he said:

"You know what, Peanut? You and I will start us a little garden. Faith! And why did I not think of that before?" His eyes went dreamy with a far-away look in them as he went on: "A wee patch of grass with bulbs planted on the edges. . . . Och, now, it is the end of August and we could see the green before the snow falls. . . ."

Peter remembered the feel of green grass in the cove.

"Can we make grass, Pat?" he asked, his own eyes shining.

Pat's laughter rumbled. "That we cannot, laddie. But we can plant the seeds and watch the miracle as the Lord makes them grow into grass. On my day off now, Sunday it is, I'll bring a man-sized spade and a rake."

Then Sunday came. Peter and his mother were sitting on the rocks by the rust-eaten fence, when a familiar big voice boomed: "Where are you, Peanut?"

Peter scrambled to his feet. "Hello there," he began his daily greeting, only the end of it didn't come out. The big man coming toward him did not look like Pat. Gone were the stiff cap and the spotless blue coat with the buttons. Gone were the white gloves and the stick. The man was dressed in shabby clothes, old hat, old shoes, and on his shoulders he carried a spade and a rake. But, as he came nearer, Peter saw the smiling broad face with the stiff

[51]

brushes for eyebrows, and finished his greeting with a ringing shout: "Pat!"

His mother rose too and stood quietly looking at Pat. Peter glanced up at her and suddenly he was glad that she had done something to her hair with soap and water early that morning. She had looked funny right after, but now the sun had dried her hair and made it into a yellow fuzz that blew softly around her face.

"She is my mother," Peter said proudly. Pat was looking at her too. He took off his hat. They both seemed surprised or scared or something, because both of them just stood and waited as Peter used to when he was still afraid of things. So he said: "Say: 'Hello there, Pat,' Mother, and ask him to sit down and rest his feet."

It was the right thing to say. They began to laugh. Pat stood very straight and said: "John Patrick O'Flanahan is the name. Patrolman of the district, off duty on a beautiful Sunday mornin'," and laughter was bubbling in her voice when she said: "Sit down, Mr. O'Flanahan, and rest your feet."

At the sound of laughter Pal came trotting from somewhere. He waited until the big man he knew to be a friend and the pale, quiet woman who fed him secretly every dawn were sitting and talking, with Peter wedged between them. Then he lay at their feet and swept the rock with his wagging tail to express his approval, dog-fashion.

Six Sundays later they stood together, Peter, his mother, Pat, and

Pal, around a little square of lawn. It was hidden by walls of rubbish that Pat had thrown aside; a secret garden no one knew about
but those who made it. Pal knew it was a secret too. He guarded
it, dog-fashion. If any of the rough boys came near the yard, Pal
made himself go ugly and yellow-eyed again and his much-stroked
smooth coat stood up in angry bristles.

The pale October sun made soft green velvet out of the tender
growth. Peter stood looking at it, one hand in Pat's huge but gentle
grip, the other clinging to the workworn fingers of his mother.
Inside his head half-formed thoughts were buzzing; he was trying
to hold one long enough to give it the wing of words. The grass
was beautiful, he knew that. Being between his mother and Pat,
holding their hands, was good. But what he felt was more than
good and beautiful. Somehow this feeling too seemed to have
grown out of the tiny seeds that Pat had planted.

Then his mother spoke; what she said was his own buzzing
thought with wings on:

"Those seeds you brought, Pat . . . they were not only seeds of
grass. They must have been seeds of loveliness and . . . content-
ment too . . . and seeds of hope."

"The laddie started it," said Pat simply, "with his little red
spade."

She smiled. "And *you* brought the spade."

"That I did not!" exclaimed Pat, surprised. She looked surprised too.

"Who did, then?" she asked Peter. His heart began to thump. He could not speak of King Peter. King Peter was a secret all his own; no one could see him but he, Prince Peter. He swallowed hard and told the truth, but not all of it: "I found it in the yard."

"A brand new thing like that . . ." said his mother in a puzzled voice.

Pat shrugged. "Must have been thrown out by accident and brought here with a load of junk." He put a finger under Peter's chin and looked into his face, smiling. "All the red has rubbed off it now onto the laddie's cheeks. Finders, keepers, aren't we, Peanut? I found me a treasure too, on the dump."

"You *did*, Pat? What is it?" asked Peter.

"I am not telling," was all he said in words, but his eyes could not keep the secret. So Peter knew the answer and rubbed his cheek against Pat's sleeve.

They walked back to their favorite place on the rocks and sat in the autumn sun. There was again a lot of grown-up talk between Pat and Peter's mother, as there had been since the first Sunday. At first their talks were paths that led to things in the past. Peter listened and let their words paint pictures for him or refresh old ones he dimly remembered. The white house under the friendly trees and the strong, kindly man who had been Daddy. The time he died and afterwards, when Peter and his mother were alone. Phrases like "hospital bills" and "expensive doctors" meant very little to Peter; only a dim picture of himself, very small, in a white

[55]

room surrounded by men dressed in white and a lot of hurt where now his foot was lame.

Later, the word-paths turned from things in the past and led to things that were to come. These paths were not easy to follow; Peter often got lost. This sunny Sunday in October she spoke of school for Peter, books to feed his mind and toys for him to play with. These were just words; he didn't know what they meant. But all these things would come, she said, when once again they would live in a clean, white house surrounded by a garden under the friendly trees, far away from the smells and junk of Shantytown.

When she said that, Peter turned to cast a peek at the houses. There was a little ache in his heart; he wasn't sure that he wanted to go away from them.

Once he had been afraid of their dark faces and dull eyes of windows. But since he had seen them turn into a castle, his golden castle, he had not been afraid. He loved them for what they might be again some day.

"Can't *we* make the houses clean and white?" he asked timidly. His mother shook her head and smiled. "Only a miracle could change these, small Peter," she said.

Peter thought this over. After a while he said slowly: "Pat said that word about the grass . . . miracle. Can't we plant seeds and watch the miracle as the Lord makes the houses clean and white?"

They didn't answer. He looked up. Both Pat and his mother were gazing far away and their eyes looked funny, as if they had been

crying. So he let the question go unanswered. King Peter would come again some day, and he would ask him to make the houses clean and white next time, instead of gold like a castle. Maybe King Peter could bring friendly trees too, the way he brought the spade. Maybe he would. Even one tree would do. He would show King Peter the secret garden and ask him to put the tree where it would shade the grass. Then he would wait and watch every day, and when the tree was there and the houses were clean and white, he would lead his mother and Pat into the yard and proudly say that strange word both had used:

"A miracle from the Lord."

Planning, he fell asleep and saw what was to come.

A House for Peter

From that day on Peter began to look for King Peter. He watched the river from the ledge; boats came and went, but none of them carried his friend. He listened to the whistling autumn winds, but they never whistled the merry tune. He fought down his fear of the roaring, snorting black train monsters and walked right up to the tall, new black-painted fence every time a train went by; but none of them brought King Peter. He knew that trains carried people; he could see their faces through the windows of the cars. He didn't think that people on the trains were happy. Their faces seemed sad or angry as they frowned at Shantytown. Sometimes he waved and smiled to make them happy, but they didn't even look at him. Except one, a boy.

It happened on a stormy, rainy afternoon in late November. His mother wasn't home yet and Pat had left long ago. Peter heard the train's whistle and he went out to the new fence. The train was coming slowly through the pouring rain. By the time it reached Shantytown, Peter was very wet. Little cold rivers of rain trickled down his neck, ran all the way down under his clothes and into his shoes. It was bad, standing in the rain and getting wet, but not as bad as sitting alone in the dark room where the wind in the chimney howled angrily.

The train stopped. Through a lighted window just above him Peter could see a boy. The boy was looking at him. Peter smiled a little. The boy smiled back and waved. He was saying something. He was a nice boy; Peter liked him. But then a man and a woman

came to the window. They seemed sad and angry, looking at Shantytown right over Peter's head. The train began to move again and Peter took a few steps along the fence. The boy kept smiling at him until the train took him away. Peter went slowly back to the house and sat by the fire Pat had made in the stove before he left. The fire dried his clothes, and the room did not seem so dark now. The strange boy had left a smile that shone like a light in Peter's heart.

Next day the wind blew the clouds away. Pat came earlier than usual; he must have hurried, because he was puffing like a train. He carried a large paper bag. He was smiling all over his face. While he was fixing the fire in the stove, Peter peeked into the bag. He made a face. "Dirty onions."

Pat laughed: "Don't you be insulting me bulbs, laddie. They are tulips and jonquils, to bloom in the spring. You and I will plant them today."

"Why not Sunday?"

"Because they are a surprise for your mother, that's why. Can you keep a secret?"

Peter was sure he could. He had one of his own to keep—King Peter. He nodded.

"Yes, Pat."

They planted the bulbs in four straight rows around the patch of lawn. Pat dug deep little holes, showed Peter how to put a bulb in each, and then together they covered them up. It took a long time and when the last hole was tightly packed, Pat had to leave.

"You stay in the house now, Peanut," he said; "the wind sure has teeth today. Winter is just around the corner," he sighed, buttoning all the buttons on his coat. Peter went into the house after Pat left and warmed his chilly fingers by the stove. The sun crept around the house and peeked through the dusty windows. "Come on out, Peter," it seemed to say. The wind whistled down the chimney. "Go on out, Peter," it seemed to whistle. There was a scratching sound on the door; it was Pal, saying dog-fashion: "Come on out, Peter." Pat had said: "Stay in the house," but he was only one against so many calls, so Peter had to go. And when he opened the door, he knew what wind, sun, and Pal were trying to tell him. From the yard came the sound of King Peter's merry tune.

Peter ran as fast as his lame foot would let him. Into the yard, around the bulky shape of the rusty stove and straight into the arms of the man who was King Peter, his friend. King Peter held him for a moment, then he said:

"You frightened me, boy. I thought nobody lived here any more."

"I do," said Peter with twinkling eyes, remembering the spring day when they met. "In there," he added, pointing behind him to the houses. King Peter nodded. He sat down crosslegged on the ground, facing the patch of lawn. He had made a small heap of twigs, rags, and papers and now he held a match to it. The fire flared up.

"I am cold," he said, rubbing his hands together.

"So am I," said Peter, playing the game. King Peter untied the string that held his coat together where buttons should have been, and spread it out like a tent.

"Sit down."

Peter crawled under the coat. It closed around him like a tent, shutting out the wind. He could see the sweet patch of lawn beyond the friendly fire. He could not hear the wind, only King Peter's voice saying quietly:

"It is a beautiful garden. But now you need a tree."

His simple words opened a path for Peter on which he could walk right into his sunlit dream of clean, white houses surrounded by a garden. He closed his eyes to make the dream picture shine brighter. He knew he had to talk, to use many, many words to make King Peter see the dream. He tried. Stumblingly first, then faster and faster the words came, they swarmed, then fell into place, and the dream picture grew. He told of Pat, the seeds he brought, how they grew, and how his mother's eyes shone when first she saw the green. He spoke of what he heard her say about things that were to come.

He spoke of all the things he had done and seen and felt since he had found the spade; he used up all the words he knew, even those he had heard but not understood. At last he had no more to tell, only to ask:

"Please, King Peter, make the houses clean and white, and please bring a tree."

[64]

"I will bring you a tree," said King Peter. Peter sighed a deep sigh that left him light and happy inside. "It has to be . . . right here, where you have built the fire!" he exclaimed after a hasty peek outside the coat. Then he smiled up at King Peter.

"Bring it tomorrow?"

"Not tomorrow, Peter. Next time I come," said King Peter, smiling.

"And the houses . . . ?" Peter hardly dared to ask for more, now that the dream tree had turned into a promise he knew would be kept. King Peter hesitated, but only for a moment. Then he said:

"After the tree is here, this will be a real garden . . . alive with things that grow, fragrant with the freshness that only trees, grass, and flowers can bring to a place. Then, one day, the houses will open their window-eyes and see the garden; they will open their doors and breathe in the fragrance of it. And then they will feel sort of ashamed of looking so ugly and old; they will begin to whisper and sigh and creak, to tell the people whom they had given shelter to, to make them clean and white. Maybe people will understand what the houses will tell them . . . maybe they won't. All we can do, small Peter, is to plant the tree and wait."

Peter thought he would use the strange word he had learned and see if it fitted into his dream. "Wait for the . . . miracle, King Peter?"

It was the right word. King Peter held him closer and said:

"Yes, Prince Peter. Wait for the miracle."

[65]

The fire had burned down. King Peter shivered a little. "Now I must go. I will have to go far to find the right kind of tree for you. I will go into the woods and walk from tree to tree. I will ask every one: 'Are you Prince Peter's tree?' Then one day one of them will sigh in the breeze and whisper: 'I am Prince Peter's tree.'

"Then I will have to ask: 'Do you want to leave the woods and go to where you will be the only tree in a little garden?' And the right kind of tree will whisper: 'Yes, I do.'"

"Then you will bring it?" asked Peter with shining eyes.

"Then I will bring it. And in the meantime, you can make room for its feet. Every day when the sun shines, you can dig here, where the fire was today; dig around and around to make a hole like a cup . . . a cup so big and deep that Pal could curl up in it and go to sleep. Will you do that for the tree?"

"I will," said Peter, giving promise for promise. "Could I start right now?"

"You could," said King Peter and let him go. When Peter came back with his spade, King Peter was not in the yard. He looked around, he listened for footsteps, for the merry tune; he even asked Pal: "Where is King Peter? Go find him!"

But Pal dropped his ears and his eyes went sad and helpless as he looked at Peter to say, dog-fashion:

"I am only a dog. I do not always know the paths on which a king in disguise is walking."

[66]

"Dig every day when the sun shines," King Peter had said. Maybe the sun had heard him too, and maybe the sun too had wanted a tree to play with in the yard, because it was shining every day. It did the best it could to keep winter from coming too soon.

December came gently. Days slipped by quickly for Peter. He was never alone now. He had his spade to work with, his dog to help him dig. On weekdays Pat never failed to come, to make a fire in the stove for Peter, to fill the small room with his rumbling laughter and his tales of many things.

Somehow the preparation for the tree got to be a secret too.

On the Sunday after Peter had begun to dig his big cup-of-a-hole, Pat told Peter's mother: "I will not be coming on Sundays for a while. The captain is after making a sergeant out of me and . . . it will be studying on Sundays that I will be doing."

"A sergeant!" exclaimed Peter's mother. "How wonderful, Pat! But . . . we will miss you on Sundays. . . ."

Pat drew Peter between his knees and said, looking at her over Peter's head:

"I will be remembering Sundays too . . . and maybe . . . some day . . . there will be Sunday for us every day."

She smiled. Then they walked to the yard, to look at the garden all together once more. She noticed the hole, although it was not very big.

"So that's where you and Pal get covered with mud!" She laughed. "What is it for, small Peter?"

Pat answered before Peter could. "To dream over, that's what. Myself, a wee lad in Ireland, could build castles of mud and dream them full of fine people and myself the finest of them all. Och, now . . . it is natural for men like us to go grubbing and dreaming dreams . . . isn't it, Peanut?"

Peter nodded. It was nice to be called a man like Pat. But it was much nicer that they did not find out his secret.

Days came and went their way; mild, mellow December days. At last the hole was big enough for Pal to curl up and go to sleep in. And still winter kept lurking around the corner. Each night it tried to sneak into the yard; Peter could see where its cold feet left sparkling ice on the moist spots. But each morning the sun chased it back into its dark hiding place.

Then it was the day before Christmas. It was a Sunday; Peter's mother was home. She cleaned their room and Peter helped her; she washed and ironed their few clothes; she even scrubbed Peter in a small tub of water near the stove. In the evening, after the supper dishes were cleared away, she spread a clean cloth on the table and on it placed their only lamp. "To light in the Christ Child . . . if he can see such a poor light," she said, with a sigh.

[69]

"Read to me about the Christ Child again, Mother," asked Peter. "About the stable and the shepherds who found him. . . . I'll get the book."

He brought the book she always kept by their bed. The pages were frayed around the edges from daily use, but the story the book contained would never grow old for Peter. She drew him to her lap and they bent their heads over the open pages. She read the story; he listened and looked at the pictures. Together they followed the life of the gentle Man; the life that began in a dark stable in Bethlehem on a Christmas Eve so long ago and ended on a cross. Peter knew the story by heart; he knew that the sad picture of the Man on the cross was not the end. Quickly, so he would not have to cry, he turned the page and said: "And now He is a King who lives in Heaven."

"Yes, small Peter," said his mother, smiling, "but often He walks the earth to bring comfort to those who need Him."

"Do . . . do I need Him?" asked Peter. She held him very close and there was a little sob in her voice when she said: "Oh, Peter . . . we both do . . . so much."

Peter could keep his secret no longer. It shone inside him like a light, it wanted to come out to make his mother happy. He waited, looking again at the picture of the Man who looked like his friend. He wasn't sure now, but he tried, anyway.

"I know Him . . . He is my friend," he whispered. She did not

seem to hear. Her head bent very low. Peter waited for a long time, then he said again:

"He is my friend. He will bring me a tree."

But she was asleep and did not answer. The room was silent and the lamp was burning low. Peter slid off his mother's lap and tiptoed to the window. From the city came the far-away sound of many church bells. They sounded gay and happy, almost like a tune. His eyes grew round. It *was* a tune . . . the merry tune that always brought his friend. Then Pal scratched at the door and Peter knew. He ran as fast as his lame foot would let him; out through the door, into the dark, singing night. His heart was singing too, when he saw a light in the yard, shining like a star above the heaps of useless things. Not once did he stumble as he found his way to the secret garden. Around him was darkness he did not fear, for his eyes were gazing at a small, green tree lighted by tiny candles, and he heard his friend's voice saying:

"Small Peter, I brought your tree."

"Your tree," boomed a big bell somewhere in the city and "Peter's tree," tinkled the small ones. The tiny candles on the tree flickered; in the dark sky above, stars twinkled and all the flickering, twinkling lights were like clear little voices saying: "Peter's tree, Peter's tree, Peter's tree."

Then all the lights of tree and stars shone in Peter's eyes and his heart sang like a little bell: "My tree, my tree, my tree."

This was too much happiness to keep all to himself. He had to share it.

"I want to call my mother!" he shouted, suddenly laughing.

"She is coming," said King Peter's voice. "Listen!"

From the darkness behind Peter, his mother's voice was calling: "Peter . . . small Peter . . ." and much louder rumbled Pat's big voice: "Peanut . . . laddie, where are you?"

"Look at my tree!" shouted Peter to guide them. Their faces seemed dark and tight with worry as they came running into the secret garden. Candlelight touched their faces gently, changing tight worry into soft wonder. Then his mother's arms were around Peter and Pat stood still beside them, his arms clutching packages he had brought for Christmas. He stood gazing at the tree, his mouth a round O of surprise. The packages dropped unheeded to the ground under the tree, as he reached up slowly to remove his hat. Peter's mother looked up at him with a smile shining through happy tears.

"Thank you, Pat," she said.

He only shook his head slowly and whispered: "I didn't bring this. . . ."

"Who did, small Peter?" his mother asked. Peter turned in her arms, his hands spread out: "My friend."

There was no one behind him. King Peter had gone.

[74]

"King Peter!" he cried, struggling free of his mother's arms. "King Peter, King Peter!" echoed the old houses. "King Peter!" boomed the bells. Then there was another sound. A window opened and a voice called out: "What is going on? . . ." and stopped abruptly. Another window opened, then more. And then a door creaked, one that had been closed against the yard for so long that now it cried out in protest. A shadowy figure appeared, walking slowly toward the light. It was a man, old and pale. After him came a woman, holding a ragged shawl around her. More doors opened. One by one the people who lived in the houses came out of the darkness to stand silently around the little tree, to gaze with unbelieving eyes at the secret garden none of them knew about. They were silent, yet they were strange shadows no longer, but people whom Peter did not fear. Their faces were pale and tired; their clothes were poorer than poor, but their eyes were soft and their feet very careful not to tread on the small patch of grass, still green.

There were the rough boys; only now their sharp, shifting eyes were round and smiling. One of them said: "Gee! A Christmas tree with candles! Where did it come from?"

Peter smiled at him. "It is my tree," and their eyes turned toward him round and respectful. "What do you know," one of them whispered, "the little lame kid has a tree!"

There were men, old and bent.

One tall, his white hair uncut so long that now it almost touched his shoulders. Another, whose untidy beard bristled around his deeply scarred face, and one, whose snow-white, tightly crimped hair surrounded a face that was as dark as the night.

There were men not so old, but just as bent, their shoulders hunched under ragged coats. There were women, old and almost young, huddled in shawls or coats that were far too large. One of them held a baby under her shawl. Slowly she knelt down by the tree and held the baby so that the candles shone on its tiny face. The baby gurgled and reached out toward the bough. The woman looked up at small Peter, with eyes that held a timid question, and Peter answered:

"It is *our* tree."

All faces, young and old, now turned toward him and all the softly smiling eyes seemed to say: "Thank you, small Peter."

All the bells in the city, big and small, were booming now, for it was midnight and Christmas had come. And then the old man with the long white hair lifted his face to the sky and his trembling old voice rose in a song:

"It came upon the midnight clear,
That glorious song of old. . . ."

A young voice soared:

> "From angels bending near the earth,
> To touch their harps of gold. . . ."

And then the secret garden rang with voices, young and old, and the old houses sang, echoing the words:

> "Peace on the earth, good will to men,
> From heaven's all-gracious King,
> The world in solemn stillness lay,
> To hear the angels sing."

Silence fell upon the secret garden that was secret no longer. After a long while Pat's deep, husky voice broke the silence as he said:

"Merry Christmas, friends . . . and may God bless you all."

Forever after, the memory of that Christmas remained in Peter's heart. It was a treasure he shared with all the people who lived in Shantytown. They were the same people he used to fear; they were just as poor, just as careworn, but no longer were they like silent shadows. They were friends who had learned to share the little they had and who were beginning to hope for better days to come. That Christmas night their hearts, closed for so long against love and laughter, had opened in the song they sang together; their eyes, used only to ugliness, had seen beauty that night and wanted more.

And so, although the kindly sun could keep winter no longer in its dark hiding place, the yard was not silent any more. It screamed and creaked and groaned with the protesting voices of useless junk being dislodged. Carefully, so as not to disturb the little tree and the patch of grass now sleeping under a blanket of snow, men and boys worked in the yard. They sang and whistled as they cleaned the yard and carted the ugly junk away. Day by day, as winter wore on, the piles of empty tins, old springs and beds and stoves, grew smaller and smaller. Now all the window-eyes of the old houses could see the tree; and the window-eyes began to sparkle, because the women had cleaned them. Through the clean glass, winter sun peeked into the rooms. It found every corner, and it seemed to say: "My, what dirty rooms!" So women, old and almost young, went after the dirt inside and chased it with mops and brooms.

Evenings they gathered in the room where Peter and his mother lived. No one seemed so very tired now, not even Peter's mother. They sat around the stove; the women sewed and mended, the men talked of work they would get in the spring. But somehow, as weeks went by, jobs came before the spring did. Perhaps because the men, their clothes clean and mended, walked straight and proud and were not afraid to ask for work, they found jobs more often than before.

Not afraid. No one seemed to be afraid of anything now. The ugly rats Peter used to fear left with the ugly junk they used to hide in. The cats did not seem so wild now that they were fed scraps of food and given a kind word or two. The big boys, just as rough and loud as before, were rough with the empty tins and scrap iron embedded in the frozen ground; to them it was a game as good as any other, to wrestle a stubborn piece loose, then carry it to the junkdealer for a few cents. Or to make a bonfire of rags and sweepings and dance around it yelling and shouting. Sometimes Pat helped them, so they accepted Pat as a friend.

The icy winds of winter howled just as angrily as before, but now there always was one room in one of the houses where there was a friendly fire, hopeful talk, and often song and laughter louder than the wind.

It was a cold winter and a fierce one. It raged and howled, it blew ice and snow over everything; but snow meant work for the men, cleaning the city streets. Work meant food and warm rooms at the end of day; work well done meant maybe a steady job later on. So each dawn the men left for the city, but now they did not go alone; they went marching off together, whistling in the face of the wind. At night they tramped back, tired and cold but seldom with empty hands.

Then spring came. Not all of a sudden; it had to fight winter off. But the sun, hidden and helpless for many weeks behind heavy clouds, was riding high again and it was helping spring against winter. By the end of March they won the fight, spring and the sun.

They swept into Shantytown together and went to work. The sun warmed the small patch of grass and spring painted it green again. The sun danced around the little tree and spring stuck tiny pale green candles of fresh growth on every bough. The sun tapped with shining fingers on the windows of the old houses, and when they were opened spring marched in. It just said "Hello," but could not stay because there was so much to do outside, so people followed spring into the yard and began to plan.

Visions of a real garden that would fill the yard with green and blooming things began to grow in their hearts. They saw themselves and the ones they loved in the dream garden and they smiled at what they saw. Each one had a dream and each one thought he was the only one who dared to dream of happiness and beauty in Shantytown. But spring and the sun can see growing things even if they are dreams hidden in people's hearts. And maybe the sun said to spring: "You get them into the yard all together and I will coax those dreams out of their hearts."

[83]

Maybe that is how it happened that on Easter Sunday Pat marched into Shantytown and shouted like a boy:

"Hey, Peanut! Look at your friend, the Sergeant!"

Everyone heard him and everyone came running into the yard.

Small Peter was the first to reach him. Pat picked him up, unmindful of the small muddy shoes that left streaks of dirt on his brand-new coat. His brand-new cap was knocked awry, but Peter was rubbing a cold little nose against his freshly shaved cheek like a loving puppy, so Pat only chuckled. He shook hands with the men and women surrounding him. Each had a kind and joyful word to say about his success. He smiled at them one and all in answer. Then he whispered into Peter's ear:

"Anything showing yet?"

Peter nodded, his eyes brimming with laughter. "I just looked. They are just . . . so big." He showed Pat the very tip of his little finger. "All of them!" he added, almost shouting.

"Praises be!" chuckled Pat. "This is almost as good as getting my sergeant's stripes. Come on, everybody. Peanut and I have a surprise for you."

He led the way to the patch of grass and pointed proudly. "Look now; we planted bulbs in November and now, in a little while, there will be flowers around the grass."

They looked. Bravely pushing up through the heavy earth, tiny sprouts of green stood around the grass like a midget fence. Reuben, the old colored man, knelt down and touched one after another with a trembling, very gentle finger. He looked up at Pat, his face full of wonder: "I . . . I used to be a gardener," he said slowly, perhaps as an explanation for the trembling of his hand and the tear that he blinked away.

The woman who had the baby—Mary was her name—smiled at her husband. "Remember, Bill," she said, "the row of yellow jonquils along the path on your father's farm?" Bill reached for her hand. "We should never have sold it," he sighed.

John, the old man with the long white hair, spoke: "There is a way back for you . . . you are young. I am too old to begin again. Shantytown is the end of the road for me." Then he shook his head and smiled. "But Shantytown with jonquils blooming in the yard is not a bad place, after all."

No one said anything for a while. A light breeze had come up from the river and danced, whispering, through the yard. The old houses drying out in the warm sun and the breeze sighed and creaked. Suddenly Peter remembered King Peter's words: "The houses will open their window-eyes and see the garden . . . they will begin to whisper and sigh and creak, to tell the people whom they had given shelter to, to make them clean and white. . . . Maybe the people will understand. . . ."

Then old John was speaking again, his eyes on the houses. "Not a bad place at all. I can still see the noble lines of these old houses, through the dirt and neglect. Good houses they used to be. . . . I know. I used to be a carpenter, a good one too," he added.

[85]

Mike, the man with the deeply scarred face behind the bristling beard, blinked up at him, then at the houses. He chuckled. "You have nothing on me, brother. I used to be a painter. Give me a few gallons of paint and a brush . . . what I couldn't do with these houses!"

Peter's heart was pounding. "White paint?" he asked and his voice squeaked a little in his excitement. Mike laughed. "White paint, boy . . . and blue for shutters. . . ."

"Or green . . ." said old John, hesitantly. "Some putty, a few panes of glass . . ."

"That's my job," said Mike. "I am the painter. The steps need mending and all the boards are loose. You see to it that everything is tight before I put the first coat of paint on. Come on"—he grabbed old John by the arm—"I want to show you what I mean!"

They walked to the nearest house, absorbed in their argument. Bill smiled at Mary. "We could have that vegetable garden down by the fence . . ." he began, but Aunt Sarah, one of the older women, broke in: "Oh, no! I want hollyhocks along that fence . . . or maybe a rambling rose or two. The vegetables should go way down into that corner, where the sun can get at them all day. . . ."

And now, all their secret dreams were coming out into the sunshine. They planned, argued, walking back and forth, each adding a fragment to the other's dream. Old John was the first one to come back to reality. His argument with Mike had grown loud, when suddenly he stopped in the middle of a sentence and looked around

His shoulders sagged again and his smile was sad. "We all must have a touch of the sun. Why . . . we can't do a thing. This . . . this is Shantytown and we are only squatters in nobody's houses. . . . What right have we to dream?"

His words were like a dark cloud hiding the sun. People looked at one another and all their eyes held the question: "What right?" They were silent because none of them knew the answer.

Peter looked from one to another. All the smiles were gone; even his mother looked sad. Pal, who had been running and barking among the people, so happy a moment ago, now pressed his head against Peter and whined, to ask, dog-fashion, what had made them so silent again. Pat was looking far away, with a thoughtful frown on his face. And small Peter, who wanted to do something to save his dream, did not know just what to do. Only King Peter could help now, he thought, but King Peter wasn't here; he had not been here since he had brought the tree.

Peter never knew why he began to whistle the merry tune; perhaps because he wanted his friend to come. On the verge of tears, he whistled alone in the sad silence around him. And then old John lifted his head. He looked at Peter oddly. He began to hum, and slowly words were shaping themselves to King Peter's merry tune:

"Oh . . . come . . . all ye . . . faithful . . . joyful and triumphant. . . ."

No one else seemed to hear, because Pat's big cheerful voice broke in: "I've been thinking, John. Sure—these are nobody's houses. I

[88]

know. I found that out this winter. The last owner died fifty years ago and no one has paid taxes on this place since. They just got to be Shantytown because nobody wanted them. The city owns them, but to the city they're not worth even tearing down. That's what the men in the City Hall said. They won't be bothering you here . . . they never have. So, look here. If you want to do a little fixing and painting, I'll say a good word in the city for you and . . . maybe I can get the loan of some tools and paint. . . ."

Nobody answered. They only looked at him, but there was a promise of a smile on most faces. Peter closed his eyes and kept whistling. Pal sniffed the air and gave a joyful bark, as if he were welcoming someone no one else could see.

Pat cleared his throat and went on: "Some of you have steady jobs now. Most of you work off and on. . . . Och, now, I'm not much for pretty talk, but there is not one among you who is not a man after me own heart. Kicked around by life you were, sure. Only, I am the cop on the beat and I know that there is not one among you who has asked for charity or gone around whining for a dime he didn't earn. Proud you are . . . poorer than poor but proud, and I . . . I am indeed the proud man to know you."

He took off his cap and wiped his forehead as if the long speech had been very hard work. Slim, one of the rough boys, was the first to speak. He said, in an awed voice: "Gee . . . you are a swell guy, Pat!" Then he looked at his companions. They nodded. So Slim took a deep breath and said: "We . . . sort of been thinking too,

[89]

my pals and I, and look, Pat, we got some money for the junk. We were going to spend it on movies or something. But . . ." He couldn't go on, simply stood hanging his head and looking at his feet.

"Go on, Slim." Young Joe nudged him. Slim blinked at Pat. "Aw, it's sissy stuff . . . but anyway, we thought it would be more fun to . . . aw . . . to buy grass-seed and make a lawn." He jerked his chin toward the little patch of grass. "Bigger than that . . . postage-stamp there. So . . ." He held out his hand to Joe and Jack and said gruffly: "Come on now, give me the dough before I change my mind."

He fished out his own pennies too and held out the small handful to Pat. "Go on, take it. We earned it," he declared, frowning, when Pat hesitated. "You . . . maybe you can get more for it than we could."

Pat slipped the money into one pocket and brought a big white handkerchief out of the other. He blew his nose hard and muttered: "Must be getting a cold. . . ."

"Never mind, Pat," said Peter's mother, with a smile, "we are all sniffling with your kind of cold." Her face grew serious, then she looked slowly around the yard, at the tree, the sprouting promise of flowers, at the faces of people whom now she knew so well. She looked after the three boys who were now running across the tracks, yelling like young Indians. Speaking almost to herself, she said: "It would be a shame to leave now, when a new spring

is just beginning. . . ." She faced Pat and laid her hand on his sleeve. "Pat, you wanted us to leave Shantytown and I said we would, as soon as my debts are paid. They will be, next month. I could pay rent for a little room some place. But . . . I would . . . I would rather help to make that lawn and to grow those hollyhocks . . . and to"—she smiled down at Peter, whose face was shining— "to make these houses clean and white."

Pat was looking at Peter too. He bent and lifted him high onto his shoulder. "Praises be," he chuckled, "I see that I will have to get a little paint brush for Peanut, to let him finish what he has started with his little spade."

Spring was reluctant to leave the yard that year. There was so much to do, so much to see. Every dawn the sun pointed long, shining fingers this way and that, and every morning there was something fresh and gay and new to see where only ugliness had been before.

By May the tulips and the jonquils stood long-legged and graceful around the little lawn and, when the breeze danced through the yard, they swayed with the breeze. The rest of the yard was spaded up and raked; it lay like a smooth brown carpet between the houses. Slowly, as May went by, brown turned into green, studded with yellow stars. The yellow stars were dandelions—only weeds to those whose eyes are spoiled by too much beauty, but stars to Peter and the others in Shantytown.

[92]

Birds found the yard. Sparrows hopped about, fresh, loud and chattering, hunting for stray seeds no one begrudged them. Robins ran up and down the lawn, to pause with cocked heads and listen to the sound worms made in the ground, a sound that only they could hear.

Spring did not leave until the seeds of hollyhocks and vegetables, planted in long, orderly rows, poked green seedling heads out into the sun. Then spring had to go, but first it led summer into the yard.

"Surprise, surprise," the sun seemed to say as it played hide and seek with summer. Fluffy white clouds were racing across the sky and the sun laughed out from behind them, showing summer all there was to see.

Summer stood breathless and still on the green carpet stretching from the houses to the old iron fence. The little tree, dark, glistening green, stood guard over a home-made crib in which a baby was sleeping. The tulips and jonquils of spring were gone, but there were new plants growing between their drying stalks, young plants waiting for summer to bring them into bloom.

There were boys laughing between the rows of vegetable plants, raking and hoeing between the rows. They were working together, making a game of it, and if the smallest boy was lame it did not matter in this kind of game.

The houses stood as summer had remembered them, dark and old. But there were crude scaffolds against them and on the scaffolds two old men were working and whistling together. The sun

peeked out from behind a fluffy cloud and one of the men sighed, wiping his forehead: "Phew . . . I am wringing wet." The other man kept on, hammering a nail into a loose board. "Well, summer has come," he said, smiling.

A warm breeze rolled lazily through the yard. Maybe it was summer sighing: "Well, well . . . there is plenty to do for me here this year. Let's get to work."

And while summer worked in the yard, bringing spring's seedlings into flower, in the big city beyond the tracks people began to whisper: "There is something happening out there in Shantytown."

The whispers grew. People began to come to Shantytown. They saw the garden. They saw and heard the laughing boys and the whistling, working men. They saw the patches on the houses and looked, through shining windows, into clean rooms. They went back to the city and talked about what they had seen. "It's wonderful what those poor squatters are doing," they said, and then they were saying: "We ought to help them." A little while later "ought" changed into "will," and by that time the talk had grown so loud that even the Mayor heard it.

Summer was still in the yard when he came, with many other men, to see what was happening in Shantytown. He was a kind man and a wise one. He saw what had been done in the yard and on the houses, but, more than that, he saw what could be done. He talked to the men and women, one by one. Because he was kind and did not pry too deeply into the sad years they were trying to forget,

[96]

they answered all his questions. Because he was wise, he did not have to pry; the past was gone, and wherever he looked he could see the promise of a future worthy of all the help he was able to give.

Promise bloomed in the flowers and lifted its head proudly in the little tree; promise shone brightly in the plain, honest faces of young and old. There was promise in the tools leaning against the fence and in every mended step and new windowpane on the houses.

Because the Mayor was both kind and wise, he did not make a long speech. He simply added his own promise to all those around him, as he said:

"Every one of you who has had a hand in making a garden out of the city dump, has earned the right to live in that garden. The houses and the ground belong to the city; I cannot give them to you. But I can, and will, ask every one of you to stay and work for the city, to make and keep this place as beautiful as your work and the city's money can make it."

He did not wait for an answer; he could read all their answers in their eyes.

Next day, once again trucks rumbled across the grading on the tracks; not trucks loaded with junk the city could no longer use, but trucks carrying lumber, tools, ladders, paints, glass for all the windows, barrels of nails—everything that was needed to make the sad old houses young again and bright and gay again.

Summer had left, as unwillingly as spring, and autumn was busy in the garden when the last scaffolding was torn down and the last shutter hung. Inside, the houses were still old and worn; painting the rooms and stairways would be winter work. The small church had no bell in its steeple, its empty windows were waiting for colored glass, and there were no pews inside and no altar. It did not matter. Those things would come, with time. Another spring, another summer would see all that work done. The coming winter would kill the autumn flowers now blazing in the sun; it did not matter. There were new seedlings that would survive the winter and many, many bulbs planted deep in the ground, gathering strength for another spring.

Of sad, old Shantytown nothing was left but its name. The houses were snow-white and no longer did they lean on one another for support. All their shining windows were open between blue-painted shutters. The shutters were fastened securely to the walls; they were no longer needed to hide hopelessness living in ugly rooms. The iron fence along the riverbank was once more guarding a garden. Next spring it would support the flowering shoots of rambling roses, and later hollyhocks would grow into a taller fence, flowering through the summer.

And so the day came when once again they stood together, Peter, his mother, Pat, and Pal the dog, by the little square of lawn that, not quite a year ago, had been their secret garden. The secret garden now was only a small part of a large, beautiful one that belonged to all these people whose hearts dreamed a dream and whose hands made it come true.

Peter stood looking around him, one hand in Pat's huge but gentle grip, the other clinging to the workworn fingers of his mother. Inside his head half-formed thoughts were buzzing; he was trying to hold one long enough to give it the wing of words. His dream of white houses surrounded by a garden had come true; there was even the tree. He had waited and watched for the day when at last the houses would be clean and white, so he could lead his mother and Pat into the yard and proudly say: "A miracle from the Lord."

But now the word would not be the right word to say. It had been all used up, day by day. Almost everyone had used it: Pat, his mother, the Mayor, all those strange people who had come from the city. His dream was no longer a surprise. And deep down inside him another dream was forming; he was groping for that, to give it to his mother as a surprise.

The dream had started while he watched the men who worked on the houses, while he stood listening to the strange men from the city called builders and engineers. They were the ones, he knew, who, with pencils and papers, with hammers and saws and paint, had made the sad, ugly houses into the white castles of his dream. He wanted to be like them; a man who could, with tools, build a dream. . . .

That was it. Small Peter laughed out loud, because now he had the surprise for his mother, all ready, in words. He looked up at her and said:

"When I grow up I am going to be a builder."

She did not answer. She only looked at him and then at Pat. The smile on her face was beautiful to see. It was Pat who broke the smiling silence. "Faith, and what else could he be? He, with his little spade, building castles out of the mud and dreaming them full of fine people. . . . Well"—he spread his arms wide—"here they are, for all of us to see."

Peter Marsh had finished his story. The office had grown dark; through the tall windows Thomas Crandon could see the millions of lights of the big city. For a long while he did not speak. Then he asked softly: "And King Peter?"

Peter Marsh rose from behind his desk. He switched on a light and walked to a cupboard in the corner. He was limping a little. From the cupboard he took a little spade, a toy spade, old and worn. He held it in his hands and on his face was a gentle puzzled smile. "I don't know," he said slowly. "This and the tree—that tall, beautiful pine—are all I have to prove that King Peter was not a dream. After he brought the tree, I never saw him again. He was a tramp . . . or was he? I do not know. I never told of him to any-one but you. I couldn't. But you . . . once, long ago, you left a smile in Shantytown that shone like a light in a lonely boy's heart. And so today I give you . . ."

Thomas Crandon rose. He held out his hand and Peter Marsh took it. Thomas Crandon smiled as he said:

"Today small Peter gave Tommy light for light."